WITHDRAWN
CEDAR MILL & BETHANY LIBRARIES

Topic: Interpersonal Skills **Subtopic:** Empathy

CEDAR MILL COMM LIBRARY
12505 NW CORNELL RD
PORTLAND, OR 97229
(503) 644-0043
OCT 2019

Notes to Parents and Teachers:

As a child becomes more familiar reading books, it is important for them to rely on and use reading strategies more independently to help figure out words they do not know.

REMEMBER: PRAISE IS A GREAT MOTIVATOR!

Here are some praise points for beginning readers:

- I saw you get your mouth ready to say the first letter of that word.
- I like the way you used the picture to help you figure out that word.
- I noticed that you saw some sight words you knew how to read!

Book Ends for the Reader!

Here are some reminders before reading the text:

- Point to each word you read to make it match what you say.
- Use the picture for help.
- Look at and say the first letter sound of the word.
- Look for sight words that you know how to read in the story.
- Think about the story to see what word might make sense.

Words to Know Before You Read

chirps
flock
flutter
friend
head
scared
shy
together

Fern Finds Her Flock

A Story About Friendship

BY
MEEG PINCUS

ILLUSTRATED BY
KATIE WOOD

Rourke Educational Media
A Division of Carson Dellosa Education
rourkeeducationalmedia.com

The flock chirps and chatters.

But Fern sits alone.

"She must not want to be friends," the birds say.

They take off without her.

Fern tucks her head in her wing.

Flora flies back.

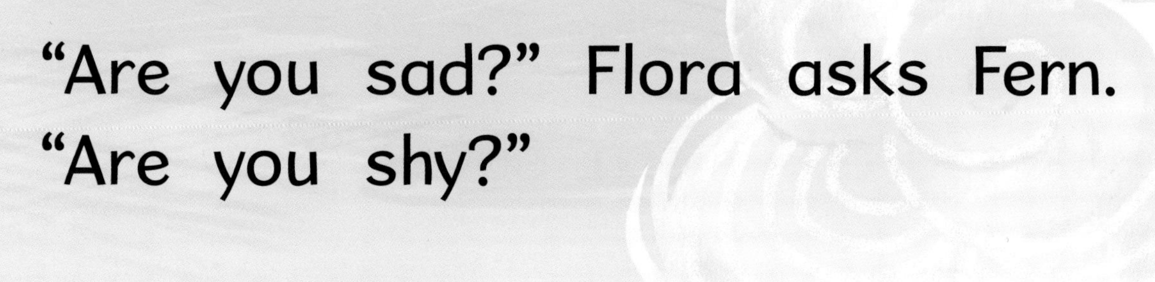

“Are you sad?” Flora asks Fern.
“Are you shy?”

“I am scared,” Fern says. “Scared to fly.”

“Let me help you,” Flora says.

They fly together.

They find the flock.

"Fern wants to be friends," Flora tells the birds.

“She just needs help to fly.”

“Oh!” they tweet.

"Of course!" they twitter.

They flutter around Fern.

They help their new friend.

Book Ends for the Reader

I know...

1. Where is Fern at the beginning of the story?
2. What does Flora do that is different from the flock?
3. How do the other birds act when they learn that Fern needs help?

I think...

1. Why do you think Flora flew back to Fern?
2. Have you ever felt left out, shy, or scared to join a group?
3. What are some ways you can make new friends?

Book Ends for the Reader

What happened in this book?

Look at each picture and talk about what happened in the story.

About the Author

Meeg Pincus has been a writer and educator for more than twenty years. She has also worked as a book editor and a Disneyland performer. She lives in California with her husband, two children, and two chirpy birds named Eddie and Iggy.

About the Illustrator

Katie Wood has always loved drawing, and with lots and LOTS of practice and studying she now works as a freelance illustrator. She has been very lucky to work on wonderful projects all over the world. Her favorite things to draw are horses, flowers, and birds! When she is not drawing, she likes to walk her playful dog, Inka, in the English countryside.

Library of Congress PCN Data

Fern Finds Her Flock (A Story About Friendship) / Meeg Pincus
(Playing and Learning Together)
ISBN 978-1-73160-590-0 (hard cover)(alk. paper)
ISBN 978-1-73160-426-2 (soft cover)
ISBN 978-1-73160-643-3 (e-Book)
ISBN 978-1-73160-663-1 (ePub)
Library of Congress Control Number: 2018967562

Rourke Educational Media
Printed in the United States of America,
North Mankato, Minnesota

© 2020 Rourke Educational Media

All rights reserved. No part of this book may be reproduced or utilized in any form or by any means, electronic or mechanical including photocopying, recording, or by any information storage and retrieval system without permission in writing from the publisher.

www.rourkeeducationalmedia.com

Edited by: Kim Thompson
Layout by: Kathy Walsh
Cover and interior illustrations by: Katie Wood